Relative

Alisia D. Bick

Contents

A heroin addict struggling with recovery finds an unusual solace in a brilliantly beautiful girl in his therapy group, who seems to have being happy and sober down to a science.

Kai Danford might be self-deprecating, self-doubting, and self-loathing, but he isn't a quitter. That includes quitting smoking two packs a day even though he can hardly breathe, and quitting dope even though he's supposed to be in recovery, and quitting his on and off again relationship with his toxic ex-girlfriend. But when Kai encounters the brilliant ray of light that is AJ Ricardi in the outpatient therapy program he's forced to attend, he's immediately smitten with her. Past all of Kai's track marks and bloodshot eyes, AJ might actually see something in him he doesn't see in himself, and when AJ offers to help Kai in his recovery, he jumps at the opportunity to spend more time with her. When romantic feelings begin to complicate their friendship, he realizes that choosing between love and drugs isn't so simple.

01

The medical definition of addiction is "a psychological and physical inability to stop consuming a chemical, drug, substance, or activity."

Personally, I think everyone is an addict.

Have you ever seen anyone go through caffeine withdrawal? My freshman year of college, my roommate decided to give up caffeine as part of some hokey Instagram "detox," and I swear he had the shakes for a week, like a junkie desperate for a hit. What followed was uglier than roadkill on a hot summer day.

Gambling addictions triggered the same exact brain areas as drug and alcohol use did, and I witnessed the hysteria of some of those guys when I went to inpatient rehab last year. Nothing made you more crazed than money (or lack of it), and they made my dope benders look like a sunset walk on the beach.

There were people who were addicted to sex. While that wasn't me, I was probably addicted to having sex with Sage Heller specifically, despite the fact that she was quite possibly the worst human being on

Earth. After years of going back and forth between her and I, I learned I wasn't really any better. That's probably why despite everything, I was still the first person she called when she came home from college for the summer. It was nearly midnight by the time I slipped through her bedroom window, and it should have felt nostalgic, but something sour sat in the pit of my stomach.

Sage's designer duffle bags still littered the plush carpeted floor of her bedroom, heaps of clothes haphazardly strewn like confetti. We filled the room with smoke before it whooshed out the open window and traded pills in each other's mouths. It ached when she kissed me, but it ached more when she didn't.

"I really did miss you."

I exhaled smoke out of her window before turning myself back around on her cushioned window seat. She sat up in bed, working her fingers through her sex-swept mess of hair. The light of the moon turned her bloodshot eyes to crystal.

"Did you?" I asked, turning back to the window and taking another hit of the blunt.

She scoffed. "Don't be like that, Kai."

Don't be like that. Sage Heller lingo for don't ask questions you don't want the answer to. I shouldn't have cared, but despite all the distance we had tried to put between us, we found ways to keep clawing our way back to each other. It wasn't like we'd be good for anyone else.

"Come back to bed." Sage patted her comforter on the open spot beside her.

I did as she asked, but I didn't sleep, my bones and my head rattling as I came down from a swirling high. I was sure by now that my body hated me and all my shit life choices and constantly found ways to remind me of that.

✗✗✗

I slipped out of Sage's bedroom before dawn, plucking my skateboard from behind the azalea bushes that lined the white lattice privacy fence surrounding their overly manicured yard. I unlocked the back gate and trudged through the sand dunes and marram grass (even though there's a thousand signs that say not to do that) until I reached the quiet haven of the beach. I'd always been told I had an addictive personality, and while I craved the normal things like dope and cigarettes, I also craved the peace of the ocean in the early mornings. Some fucking balance to keep me teetering on the edge.

I took one last look over my shoulder at Sage's house, towering on its six feet of stilts above the beach and piercing the hazy morning sky with its obnoxious shade of coral. It was a place I'd been a million times but still felt unfamiliar.

It took almost three miles and four cigarettes to get from Sage's house back to mine. At some point on my walk of shame, still dragging my skateboard and a cloud of smoke behind me, I sat into the sand and shut my eyes. Before I knew it, dawn melted into mid-morning, and I'd melted into the sand.

When you were coming off a bender and you woke up soaking wet and hot, it usually meant one of two things - you had broken a dope sick fever sometime in the middle of the night and were lucky enough to have sweated it out, or you weren't so lucky and you pissed yourself because you have no control over your body's raging war with your shitty life choices. One thing that usually didn't come along with soaking wet and hot was a hand on your shoulder and a voice in your ear that maybe, quite possibly, was an angel.

"Hey..." she shook me again, and even though she probably didn't mean to, it made the aching in my arm worse.

I tried to open my eyes, but the glare of the morning sun turned everything into a blurry mess of colors. I shut my eyes again in an attempt to soothe my pounding head, the overly pungent smell of low tide churning a storm in me. After slowly trying to adjust to the sunlight, I looked up into a pair of blue eyes so icy, I felt a real chill hit my body. Her face was tanned from the sun with a spattering of freckles, and her cinnamon colored hair was so long it brushed against my chest when she leaned over me. She wasn't the intense, manufactured beauty I was used to with Sage. She was soft, kind of like the first breeze of the morning before it got bogged down by the heat.

"You okay?" she asked in a clipped tone. There wasn't an ounce of the southern proper drawl I was used to hearing from people around here. She squinted down at me and pressed her lips into a pout, like she was trying to figure out what kind of animal I was all washed up on the beach.

"Yeah, I'm fine," I muttered, gripping sand still cold from the night between my fingers to force some feeling back into them. I heard her scoff in response.

Still in sensory overload, the smell of vanilla and coconut wafted off of her, and it made my stomach ripple. Whether it was nausea or something else got lost in the morning haze. I swallowed hard and tried to regain my focus. I managed to sit myself up, and she sat back on her knees. Her light, glass-like eyes glinted with the same silent, curious worry that I had grown used to from everyone else around our tiny beach town, but I had never seen her before. Was she someone's cousin, or niece, or half-sister, and had whispers of "that Danford kid who can't get his shit together" already reached her ears?

"Are you sure you're okay?" She tilted her head to the side, firing off words too quickly for me to process. It wasn't the usual sad pitying I was used to, but it wasn't unkind either. It was just plain curiosity. "Do you need help getting home?"

I shook my head and jerked my thumb over my shoulder. "I live right over there."

I knew without even needing to truly look around. Back in high school, I had marked a couple of big rocks by the boardwalk that led from my house to the beach when I had a short-lived relationship with graffiti. They stuck up out of the sand right behind her, the colors faded but still visible, half-coated in seaweed.

"I uh..." I cleared my throat, trying to get some life back into my mouth so I didn't sound completely strung out. "I must have just fallen asleep on my morning walk. I'm okay, really."

"Well, sorry for disrupting your nap then." She rose to her feet, brushing sand off her leggings. I expected her to turn away, but she didn't, lingering with that same curious look.

"You know..." she pinched her lips into a frown. "In theory, you're probably a really good liar."

I was so gobsmacked by her words, I felt myself tripping over my own in an effort to respond. "I'm sorry, what?"

"Your eyes," she said. "When people feel guilty about lying, it's always in their eyes."

She turned away before I had a chance to bite back (though I really didn't know what I could say at that point) and continued her run down the beach. I itched at a scab on the inside of my arm, took a deep breath and hoisted myself to my feet. Sand came flitting off my knees and my elbows, little pieces of me eroding away like the ocean stripped away the shoreline, pulling it all into the depths.

XXX

any thoughts or feelings on chapter 01 are welcome!

02

"You fucking liar. You fucking lied to my fucking face and actually thought I wasn't going to find out."

Stella was angry, and I knew that without having to look at her. My sister's voice was more identifiable than anyone else I knew - South Carolina Buttercup Princess mixed with grating nails on a chalkboard, and it slammed into me like a truck the moment I slipped through the back door. She sat on top of our kitchen island, legs swinging and sipping her standard morning cup of tea. Morning light spilled in through the series of big open windows facing our back deck, and with it came the sound of the ocean.

"You'll need to be a bit more specific." I could hear the apathy in my voice, and I didn't make eye contact with her as I fumbled over to the fridge and yanked out a bottle of Sunny D. Before I could even unscrew the cap, Stella swooped in beside me, gently taking the bottle from my hands and replacing it with a warm mug. Stella had all the grace and reflexes of a stealthy cat, and I was more like a sloth that had fallen on its head a few times.

"Drink this," she said, her voice softer than before. "You need it."

"It smells like dirt." I wrinkled my nose at it. "I don't need any of your weird beauty pageant health rituals."

She scoffed. "It's not a weird health ritual, Kai, it's fucking tea. Green tea is a detoxifier. You need to be detoxified...from several things."

She returned to her spot on the counter, legs still swinging and eyes studying me as I took a small sip, cringing as it hit the back of my throat. Not only did it smell like dirt, it tasted like dirt too.

"This still doesn't get you out of the fact that when I asked you yesterday if you were going to see Sage, you were so overdramatic when you told me no fuck off, and for a moment I actually believed it." Venom coated Stella's words, but when I looked up into her eyes, the same stormy gray as mine, hurt shrouded them like a cloud.

I groaned and set the mug down a little too aggressively, sending hot liquid splashing all over the counter and my hand. "Don't start with this shit. I don't need you pointing fingers at me, enough people do that already."

"You told me you were going to Hunter's house." She kept her narrowed eyes on me, like a lioness stalking prey.

"And I did go to Hunter's house," I replied with a shrug.

Her gaze didn't falter. She was ready to pounce. "Then why do you smell like cigarettes, incense, and Thai food?"

I was caught in her jaws. My sister had a knack for drawing blood in every argument she'd ever been in - it was part of what was going to make her a good lawyer, but it never benefitted me, since I was always the one that ended up bleeding.

"You know maybe you should just quit your summer job at the Junior League and go work for the fishing and game association instead," I said casually, watching her smirk twist into a sneer out of the corner of my eye. "I'm sure they could use more bloodhounds."

"All I'm saying is if you look up toxic in the dictionary, you and Princess Sage are right up there next to those 50 Shades of Grey people." She held up her hands in defense and shook her head.

Out of the corner of my eye, I saw a pamphlet for the local community college on the counter by our outdated landline phone that nobody used. I glanced back up at Stella, who continued to work her glare over me.

"Don't call Sage that," I groaned and dumped the tea down the drain without even trying to finish it. "And last time I checked, where I put my dick is none of your business."

Before Stella had a chance to fire back another stinger, my mother came waltzing into the kitchen, already dressed for the day and smelling like lavender.

"Both of my children are up by 8? Are pigs flying outside too?" My mother grinned and cocked an eyebrow at both of us before polishing off the pot of coffee sitting on the other side of the fridge. I turned my back to her and shot Stella a withering glare over the counter, to which she responded with an impassive shrug.

My mom had to stand on her toes to kiss my cheek, her voice soft against my skin. "How are you feeling?"

"Fine," I answered with a shrug. "I'm fine. I'm great. Really, I am."

She gave me a half smile, one that didn't quite reach the corners of her eyes. "Well that's good. I'll see you at the flower shop in about an hour, yeah?"

"Sure thing." I responded with a quick nod.

When she was out of earshot, Stella returned the glare I gave her earlier. "You know Kai, one day everyone is just going to stop caring about you. You should take advantage of it now while you still can."

✗✗✗

I took a longer than usual shower in an attempt to scrub the awkward mix of smells and sex off of me. I always had to duck in our tiny shower in the upstairs bathroom for the water to get anywhere above my chest.

After drying myself off and still faintly smelling of my Marlboro Lites and Sage's charred incense, I caught a glimpse of myself in the mirror and frowned. I had always been skinny and tall, like someone had thrown me in one of those weird medieval tourture machines, but I'd lost at least 15 pounds in the last few months, and skinny had turned into something more sickly. The bags under my eyes and creases in my forehead seemed like permanent additions to my face, and I desperately needed a haircut as my mop of dark hair took on a mind of its own. Seeing myself for what I had become, all gangly and awkward and damaged, made my stomach roll.

My arms were like a mini universe, dotted with stars of dried blood and freckles, and deep marks of reddish blue discoloration and bruises, like what I'd imagine a dying supernova looked like. I hadn't fallen back into straight heroin use in over two months, but my track marks were as fresh as if I'd shot up yesterday. I ran my hand over the bruises, and the urge itched at me, like tiny spiders living under my skin.

That was the thing about my relationship with drugs. They found ways to constantly remind me that they were there. Even when I wasn't using. Even when I didn't want to use. My addiction was like a shadow, constantly on my heels, dark and breathing down my neck. By the time I had put on a fresh t-shirt and the same pair of jeans from yesterday (since they were the only pair that fit me) and shuffled my way downstairs, Stella was already gone.

I slipped a tiny plastic bag out of my back pocket that I found lying around Sage's room last night and crushed half of a little white pill up with a spoon. I rubbed it on my gums and almost instantly felt a wave of euphoria wash over me, unraveling my insides and unhinging my skull from my neck, putting my aching head up in the clouds. Whether it was my pettiness that drove my addiction, or vise versa, I didn't know and I didn't care.

After jamming the spoon in the dishwasher and stashing the bag in an old cigar box under my bed, I grabbed my skateboard from the garage and made my way down our street and towards the tiny center of our island town. The municipal groundskeepers usually kept the palm trees and other foliage neat and trimmed on the one main road in town, but they were wild and overgrown on the side streets. Most of the branches and leaves blocked out the mid-morning sun, but sweat still trickled down my forehead and back as I rode down the street.

There were normally a lot of downsides to having your license suspended, but living on an island as small as Folly Beach, where I could stand on one edge of the island, spit, and it would land on the other side, my skateboard was enough. It wasn't like I went anywhere besides the flower shop and Sage's house. But there were different downsides to living in a small town. My "recommended removal" from the College of Charleston and two months stashed away in inpatient treatment was the only thing that happened in those two months, so it spread like wildfire. By the time I came back, the whispers had reached everyone's ears, and people shot me judging glances as I rode by them on the street and got my coffee in the morning. Every small town had a token fucked up guy, and that guy was me.

03

M y mother's flower shop used to be a dive bar once upon a time, and when she bought it, she kept the name, so the same gold script lettering of The Ordinary was still etched into the front window.

I couldn't remember a time that my mother didn't have The Ordinary, but if I had to guess, it was how she kept busy with my dad being gone all the time. Guys on Coast Guard cutters were away on average 185 days of the year. There were years he'd be home for almost every important holiday, like birthdays and Christmas, but there were years he wasn't. I'd learned to accept my father's transiency a long time ago. Did it impact me negatively? Who the hell knew. I just knew he loved the ocean, and it was why he named me Kai - from the sea.

The little bells on the door handle jingled when I walked into the shop, and I was instantly greeted by a blast of cold air. We were always slow in the mornings, so I didn't expect to see any customers, but my mother was nowhere to be found.

"Mom?" I called as I weaved my way further into the shop, the cement floor still damp with puddles from the morning sprinklers.

"Back here," she called from the back office behind the register. I snaked my way around shelves of orchids and vines of Boston fern that hung from the ceiling. Mom kept the back office neater and tidier than a hospital should be, which meant I didn't dare step foot past the threshold of the door. I'd sneeze and turn the place upside down. She looked up at me from a pile of papers on her oakwood desk, her dark eyes narrowed at me over the rim of her glasses. Her expression softened in an instant, and she returned to the papers.

They say moms have bullshit radar, but it never stopped me from dicking around, mostly because she never let on what she knew...or didn't.

"I'm going to be back here most of the day just going over some month end stuff for the books," she said, shuffling through more files. "You can handle the front for now, right?"

"Yeah, sure," I croaked out, my jaw numb and my words heavy. I needed ice water, and about 100 milligrams of modafinil before I passed out.

On my way back to the front of the shop, I picked up a lone rose from the floor that had fallen off its stem and tucked it behind my ear. Flowers had been part of my life since I was little, and I stopped caring a long time ago how un-masculine it made me. Flowers were also the first thing I truly learned to draw, and I remember sitting in the corner of the shop on a stool when I was 7 or 8 during summer break from school, watching my mom make bouquets and clutching my little sketchbook in my grubby hands. When I graduated from doodling in sketchbooks to oil painting, and playing in the sandbox turned into smoking behind the coffee shop, I still painted flowers. I needed anything that brought color into my gray haze of a life.

At this point, I just hoped the rose would hide the fact that I smelled like death warmed over, but I still drew flowers when I was bored, and I kept a sketchbook tucked away in the bar-turned-register at the back of the shop. I learned not to think too much when I sketched - sometimes I didn't even look at the page, I just let my hand do what it felt like. I had the outlines of a few roses before I realized I was drawing the silhouette of a girl - long hair made of threads of gold, and eyes as big and as bright as the sun.

The bells on the front door jingled, and when I looked up, I was staring right at my own sketch come alive. A pair of round Ray Ban sunglasses sat perched on her head, and those same bright blue eyes stared right back.

"Oh hey, it's the boy who sleeps on beaches." She brushed her hands over a few of the ferns that hung from the ceiling as she walked further into the shop. I stammered and quickly slammed my sketchbook shut, jamming it onto a shelf under the bar.

This was karma, telling me I was a shit person.

"Can you keep it down?" I hissed at her through my teeth. "I don't need the whole world knowing."

She looked me up and down, and suddenly I felt like I was burning up, despite the icy color of her eyes. She gave me a half smile, giving me a glimpse of perfect, brilliant white teeth. The kind that people in commercials for dentists had.

"So, I take it when you're not asleep on the beach, you work here?" she asked, and there was genuine curiosity in her voice past the playful smirk she wore.

"I mean I don't wear flowers in my hair because they bring out my eyes." I shrugged.

"Hey, I wouldn't judge you." She smiled wider at me, and it wasn't a coy or devious smile. She smiled like she meant it. "Anyway, maybe you can help me."

I barked out a laugh. "I've been told I'm pretty useless, but I could try."

If she thought I was being somewhat serious, she didn't show it. She half-heartedly laughed and kept smiling at me.

"Well, I'm not really a plant person." She turned away from me, giving me a breather from the heat of her gaze. She brushed her hand over a small eucalyptus plant, smiling down at it like it was a puppy or something. "I kill everything green I touch. But I figured I'm in a new place, might as well try something new. Plus, my aunt has me stashed in this bland, eggshell white guest room in her condo and I'm not allowed to paint the walls, so I need some color."

"So...you're not from around here?" I returned that half-smile she gave me, and when she looked back at me, she lit up.

"Native New Yorker." She pulled a leaf off of the eucalyptus, and it made me wince. "My whole world ended at the Hudson...until about two weeks ago, anyway."

"Oh yeah," I rolled my eyes at her. "That explains the whole talking fast and with your hands thing. Plus, you're wearing black in May."

I jerked my head at the leather jacket she had casually draped over her shoulders. Effortlessly cool in a way I could never even hope to be.

"So what?" she fired back. "I wear black all year round."

"Not here you won't." I shook my head. "Here's a tip from an island native: Summer starts in April and ends in November. It might get hot in New York, but you're on the edge of the map here. The sun hits you differently, and trust me, you'll feel it."

"Spoken like a true islander." By now she had taken the tiny pot with the eucalyptus in it and clutched it to her chest, almost as if she was afraid it would run away if she didn't hold onto it. "You can hear it in your voice too, ya know."

I cocked an eyebrow at her. "Hear what?"

"That subtle southern twang you try to hide so you sound more educated." Honesty like that normally felt sharp, but not from her. She was all sweet and soft and everything I wasn't used to. "But when you're used to hearing people pronounce things like cawfee and wudder, it's pretty obvious."

I leaned back against the bar and crossed my arms over my chest. "So, what else do you think you've got figured out about me?"

I wasn't smooth or charming by any means, but sometimes my apathy and general lack of interest in life worked to my advantage, including the ability to keep my cool around girls. But not her. She had me burning up, and I found myself more interested in her after only knowing her for a collective 30 minutes than anyone else I'd known for years. When she smiled back at me, it was like a fire that outlasted all the rain in my life.

"Well..." she took a step closer to me, and she smelled just as sweet as she sounded. "I bet that smile of yours gets you whatever you want."

When she said it like that, I couldn't stop my lips from curling up into a smile. Aloofness gone. I was sure the color of my cheeks matched the rose still tucked behind my ear.

"That depends, does it get your name?" I asked.

Without missing a beat, she extended her hand to me. "AJ."

My hands were nowhere near as soft and warm as hers, but she still smiled when I took her hand in mine. "Kai."

She beamed at me, and for a moment it was silent, but not an awkward kind of silence. The kind of silence you share with someone that you tell all your secrets too. Except she was the kind of girl that was too pure for all my secrets, and it made my chest burn.

"You uh...you look like you've taken a liking to that eucalyptus." I gestured to the pot in her hands.

"Oh, yeah it's cute and it smells nice."

I chuckled and shook my head. "Alright, well if you cut some off and hang it in your shower, the steam will release the oils from the plant. It's supposed to clear your sinuses and have anti-inflammatory properties."

A look of shock flashed across her face, as if she didn't actually think I'd know anything about plants despite working in a flower shop, but was quickly replaced by that sweet smile. "I'll keep that in mind. And um..."

AJ gestured up to the rose behind my ear. "Can I have one of those too?"

I reached up and plucked the flower from my head, twirling the stem between my fingers. "You can have this one. Bury it in sand overnight and it'll preserve it. That way even you can't kill it."

She gingerly took the rose from me and placed it in the pot with the eucalyptus. "How much do I owe you?"

I shook my head. "Nah, don't worry about it. Consider it your northerner transplant discount."

"Thank you." For once her words came out slowly, and they dripped off her lips like honey. "I guess...I'll see you around. Maybe next time you'll actually show me that drawing you were working on."

Heat tore through my body, and by the time her words really registered, she was out the door. I reached back down under the bar and pulled my sketchbook back out, running my fingers over the rough sketched outline of her hair and face. The adrenaline I didn't even realize was coursing through me finally wore off, and I found myself crashing, not just from the high, but back down to reality. Girls like her didn't belong with guys like me. I'd wreck her without even trying.

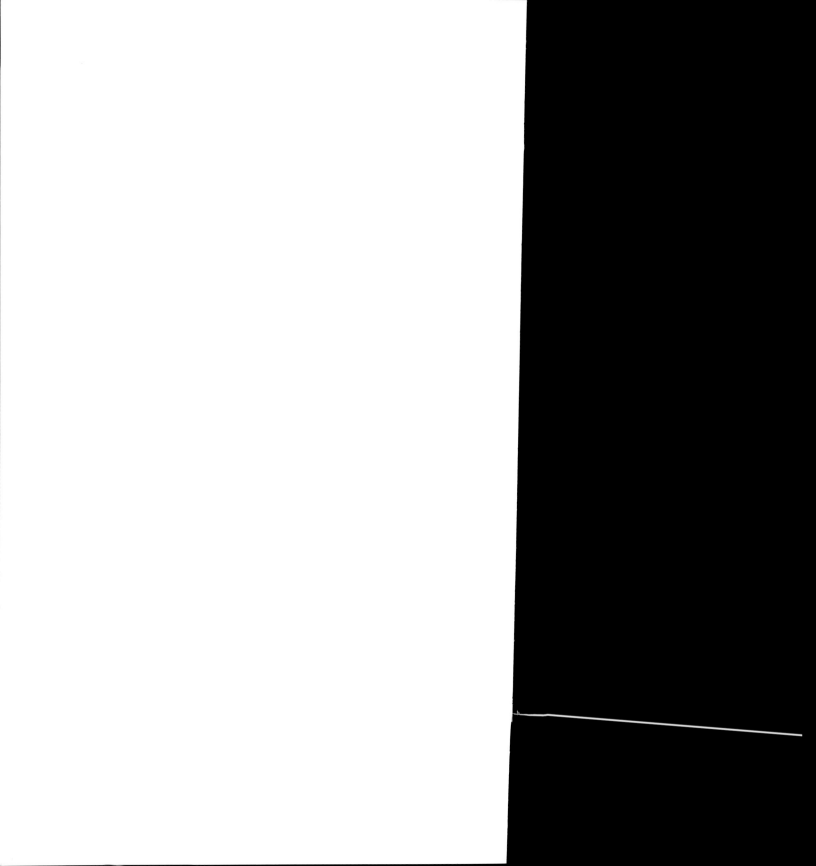

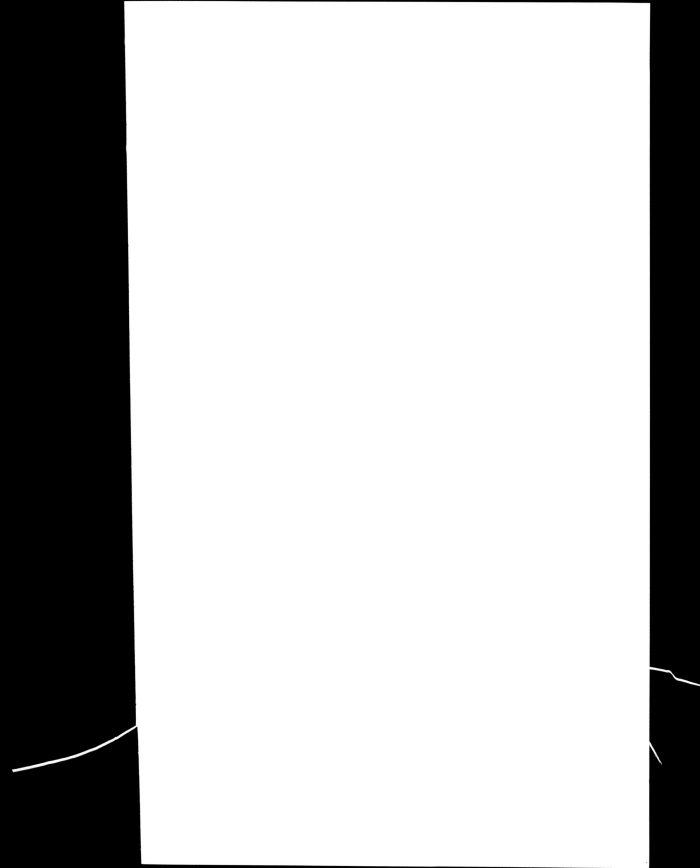

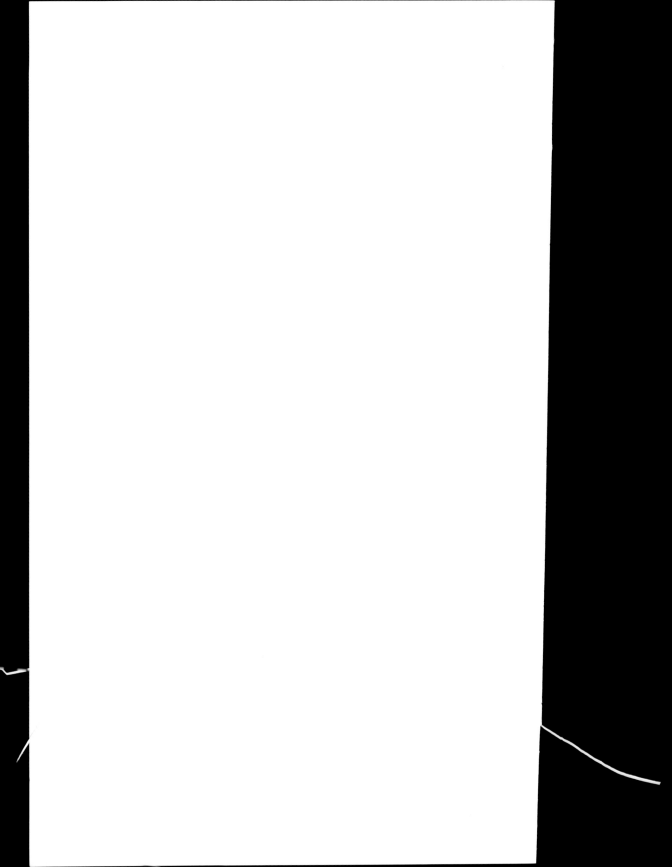